BUDDY'S BOATING ADVENTURE

STORY BY: SUZANNE SGAMBELLURI
ART BY: FARZANA ISLAM

ISBN: Softcover 978-1-7960-1610-9
Hardcover 978-1-7960-1611-6
EBook 978-1-7960-1609-3

Print information available on the last page

Rev. date: 02/25/2019

To order additional copies of this book, contact:
Xlibris
1-888-795-4274
www.Xlibris.com
Orders@Xlibris.com

For my sons Preston and Ashton who mean the world to me.

~When you feel a little tickle on your ear, know that I'm with you and know that I'm near.~

BUDDY'S BOATING ADVENTURE

Buddy loves adventures. One day Buddy and his best friend Ashton were down by the pond out their backyard. "Here, Buddy," said Ashton. "I made this especially for you."

Buddy's eyes lit up, and his tail started wagging. He loved what he saw—a beautiful paper boat.

"I made this for you because you are somebody special to me," said Ashton, giving Buddy a great big hug.

"I'm sorry I can't play with you today, Buddy. It's my friend Nathan's birthday party, and puppies aren't invited," said Ashton.

Buddy watched as Ashton walked back up the hill to their house. A tear fell down his face as he saw him drive away with his mom. It was Saturday, and Ashton and Buddy always played together on Saturdays.

Buddy was sad because he missed Ashton, but he was also very excited about his new boat. He loved playing down by the pond and loved the water.

Buddy picked up his new paper boat and sat it down at the edge of the pond. He loved how the sun shone behind it and how the shiny sparkles twinkled on the water.

Buddy lay down on the soft green grass and watched his boat floating gently. His eyes began to close, and slowly, he drifted off to sleep.

Suddenly, out of nowhere, a gust of wind came. Buddy opened his eyes and saw his boat fly up in the air. "Oh no!" said Buddy.

Buddy's boat crashed down into the pond. The wind picked up, and the ripples on the water were getting bigger. Buddy started to panic, "I have to save my ship!"

Captain Buddy held on tight to the steering wheel as his boat climbed up the big waves. The wind was getting stronger, and dark clouds started to roll in.

"Oh no! A storm!" Buddy's heart was beating fast. Hail was pounding on the top of the boat, and he could see lightning off in the distance. He had to work even harder to keep his boat from getting swooped up by the big waves.

"I have to get my boat to shore! I can't let anything happen to my special gift from Ashton!" said Captain Buddy.

Captain Buddy worked hard to keep his boat above water, steering between waves and fighting the wind. Finally, with great pride, he was able to steer clear to the shore.

The wind began to calm. The dark clouds moved off into the distance. Buddy's paper boat floated gently on the edge of the pond.

"Buddy! Buddy! I'm home, Buddy!" said Ashton. Buddy opened his eyes to see his best friend standing beside him.

"Were you sleeping the whole time I was gone, Buddy?" asked Ashton.

THE END

Meet Buddy & Ashton

This picture was taken on Caribou Island, one of the many beautiful islands off the north shore of Lake Superior. Only accessible by water, Buddy and Ashton travel by boat to visit their favourite summer getaways. They love exploring the scenic trails, watching the waves crash in and campfires by the water.

CPSIA information can be obtained
at www.ICGtesting.com
Printed in the USA
BVHW021424050319
541822BV00002B/11/P
* 9 7 8 1 7 9 6 0 1 6 1 0 9 *